For Yvonne, who is never grumpy – P B

For Dylan – J C

Copyright © 2009 by Good Books, Intercourse, PA 17534
International Standard Book Number: 978-1-56148-673-1
Library of Congress Catalog Card Number is available.
All rights reserved. No part of this book may be reproduced
in any manner, except for brief quotations in critical
articles or reviews, without permission.
Text copyright © Paul Bright 2009
Illustrations copyright © Jane Chapman 2009
Original edition published in English by Little Tiger Press,
an imprint of Magi Publications, London, England, 2009
Printed in China
Library of Congress Cataloging-in-Publication Data is available for this title

Grumpy Badger's
Christmas

Paul Bright   Jane Chapman

Good Books

Intercourse, PA 17534
800/762-7171
www.GoodBooks.com

It was almost Christmas, and the forest was a flurry of activity. The animals were bustling here and there—putting up the Christmas tree, wrapping presents, making tasty cakes and cookies—while the young ones scampered about, squeaking with excitement.

Everybody was looking
forward to Christmas.
Well, *almost* everybody . . .

Grumpy Badger looked out of his window and scowled.

"Merry Christmas!" shouted Squirrel.

"Merry Christmas? Bah!" he shouted back. "What piffle! I am a sensible creature and I sleep all through the cold winter.

"Now I am going to bed until the spring, and if anyone wakes me I shall be very, very grumpy!" And with that, he pulled his window shut with a

CLUNK!

Grumpy Badger knew he would be hungry when he woke, so he checked his pantry. There were pies and pastries, hams and cheeses, crispy crackers, jars of fruit and sticky-sweet jams.

"That *should* do," he said.

Then he filled his hot water bottle
and climbed into bed.
     He had just closed his eyes when
there was a knock at the door.

It was Mole.

"M-m-merry Christmas, Mr. Badger," he said,
timidly. "I'm sorry to bother you. I've been trying
to put lights on the Christmas tree, but it's just
too big. Could I please borrow your ladder?"

"Christmas tree?" spluttered Grumpy Badger. "Piffle and double piffle! Christmas is for sleeping—and that's what I'm trying to do!" And he closed the door with a

BANG!

"Bah!" huffed Grumpy Badger, climbing into bed. "Borrow my ladder indeed! All I want is a bit of peace and quiet, so leave me alone!"

He peeked under his bed, where he'd put more food for springtime: candies and cornbread and cherry cupcakes.

Then he cuddled deep into his big, warm comforter. He was just starting to snore when there was another knock at the door.

KNOCK!
KNOCK!
KNOCK!

This time it was Squirrel.
"Hello, Badger," he said,
cheerily. "I've brought you
a Christmas present."

"Christmas present?" snorted Grumpy Badger.

"Piffle and triple piffle!
I don't like presents and I don't like Christmas!
All I want is a little peace!" And he shut the
door with a CRASH!

Now Grumpy Badger was really grumpy. To cheer himself up, he thought about the bottles and bottles of homemade lemonade he had in the cellar. Then he lay down and closed his eyes. But he couldn't sleep—his head felt a little chilly.

Suddenly there was a loud banging at the door.

BANG!
BANG!
BANG!

"Oh, what is it *now*?" Grumpy Badger sighed. He was about as tired and grumpy as a Badger can be.

"Oh, Badger," panted Rabbit. "Help! It's poor Mole. He's stuck at the top of the Christmas tree. Come quickly!"

"PIFFLE!" shouted Grumpy Badger.
"And triple piffle on top of that!
Why can't everyone just leave me alone?" And he slammed
the door so hard that the whole house shook!

SLAM!

At long last, Grumpy Badger fell asleep.

But soon he was tossing and turning and wriggling and squirming. He was dreaming of Mole, dangling by one tiny paw from the top of an enormous Christmas tree. Mole was trembling.

Mole was about to fall!

"NOOOOOO!"
screamed Grumpy Badger,
sitting bolt upright, and
suddenly wide awake.

"What have I done?"

He jumped out of bed, grabbed his ladder
and dashed into the street.

Grumpy Badger raced up to
the Christmas tree.

"Hold on, Mole!" he cried.

He scrambled up the
ladder, scooped Mole
gently into his arms,
then helped him
down to the ground.

"I'm sorry I left you hanging,"
mumbled Grumpy Badger. "I suppose
I've been a bit of a grump."

"That's okay," said Squirrel. And he gave Badger
back his Christmas present—a soft, fluffy nightcap.

"I've been so grouchy," said Grumpy Badger.
"What can I do to make things better?"

And then he knew.

Badger's Christmas party was the best ever. There were pies and pastries, cheeses and hams and sticky-sweet jams, cookies and cupcakes and bottles and bottles of homemade lemonade.

They jigged and jived and joked and laughed, late into the night.

"Merry Christmas, everybody!" Badger cried. "And if you don't all come to my party next year,

I SHALL BE VERY GRUMPY INDEED!"